I0782222

# STANLEY

THE SPARROW

Stanley, The Sparrow
First edition, published 2022

Written by Anita Stuart
Illustrations by Melissa Hudson

Copyright © 2022

Hardcover ISBN 978-1-952685-48-4

Published by Kitsap Publishing
Poulsbo, WA 98370
www.KitsapPublishing.com

# STANLEY
## THE SPARROW

**Anita Stuart**
Author

**Melissa Hudson**
Illustrator

# Dedication

I would like to dedicate this book to my mother.

Without her love and kindness towards animals we would not have such great memories and stories to share.

Growing up in a small town in California, all the kids in my neighborhood knew that my mom worked for a veterinarian, an animal doctor.

Mom loved animals, and our house was home to many stray dogs, not to mention the three dogs we already had.  We also had many pets in our home.

We had hamsters, guinea pigs, fish tanks, birds, and even a chinchilla.

If an animal in our neighborhood got injured, the kids would always bring it to our house.

One day a boy from the neighborhood brought over a baby bird.  It was a gray and brown sparrow.

He was a young bird, only about two weeks old, and he had fallen from the nest.

Mom was not home, but we girls knew what to do. We got out the birdcage, the heating pad and mixed up some baby food.  Stanley, the bird, as we later named him, did not know how to feed himself yet.

We kept him warm and fed him until Mom returned.

She was very proud of us girls for knowing what to do and keeping Stanley safe until she arrived.

In the weeks that followed, Stanley became very attached to Mom. He thought she was his mom now too.

Still, he did not know how to feed himself.  None of us were birds and didn't know what to do.  So, Mom visited the local pet store and asked for advice.
"What should I do"?
They sold her a pair of love birds to teach Stanley how to eat like a bird.  The three birds lived together in Stanley's birdhouse, but Stanley did not like having them in his home.  He was not very nice to them.

Mom returned the birds to the pet store and explained to the store owner that it was not working out. However, in the short time they were with Stanley, they taught him how to feed himself.

We were so happy. Stanley could now eat by himself without having to depend on us.

Stanley was a happy bird. Evenings he
would fly all over the house looking for
Mom. If she watched television, he would
sit on her shoulder and watch with her.

If Mom took a bath, Stanley would call out for her, and she would say, "Stanley, I'm in here."

He would perch himself on the edge of the bathtub until she said, "Okay, Stanley, you can come in." He would jump down into the water and splash and splash until he was clean.

One time Mom had to go to a town that required passing over a bridge that had a toll, so as Mom was getting ready to go, she took some money out of her purse and put it on the counter for the toll.

She finished getting ready to go and turned to get the money she had put out.  It was gone.
Where did it go?  Who took it?
She called out to us girls and asked, "Who took the money I put out for the bridge toll?"  We all came running to see what was going on.
"I did not take it," I said.
My sisters said, "neither did I, but where could it be?"

Mom looked over in Stanley's birdhouse, and there it was.
"Now Stanley," she said, "What are you going to do with that money?  I have to go, but I will be back soon".
We all laughed and laughed.

UNITED STATES OF AMERICA
1

As the years went on, we girls grew up.  We went off
to college, got married, and had jobs.  Stanley
continued to have the run of the house most days.
He was getting older and slowing down a bit, but he still
loved his baths and television time with Mom.

One warm spring day, I called mom when I got
home from work to see how she was doing and tell her
about my day as a nurse at work.  The dogs were
playing the in-and-out game.  When they asked to go
out, then wanted right back in, so she left the door
open.   The door was often left open for the dogs.
Stanley flew right past her and went outside.

He had never done that before, but something
must have told him it was time to go.
We were sad that Stanley no longer lived with
mom, but we were happy for the time we had
with him. Stanley was able to be free.
Stanley was able to be the bird that was meant to be.

Now when I am outside and happen to see a sparrow flying free, I smile and think of Stanley.

I remember how much joy and laughter he brought into our home. I am thankful for the wonderful memories.

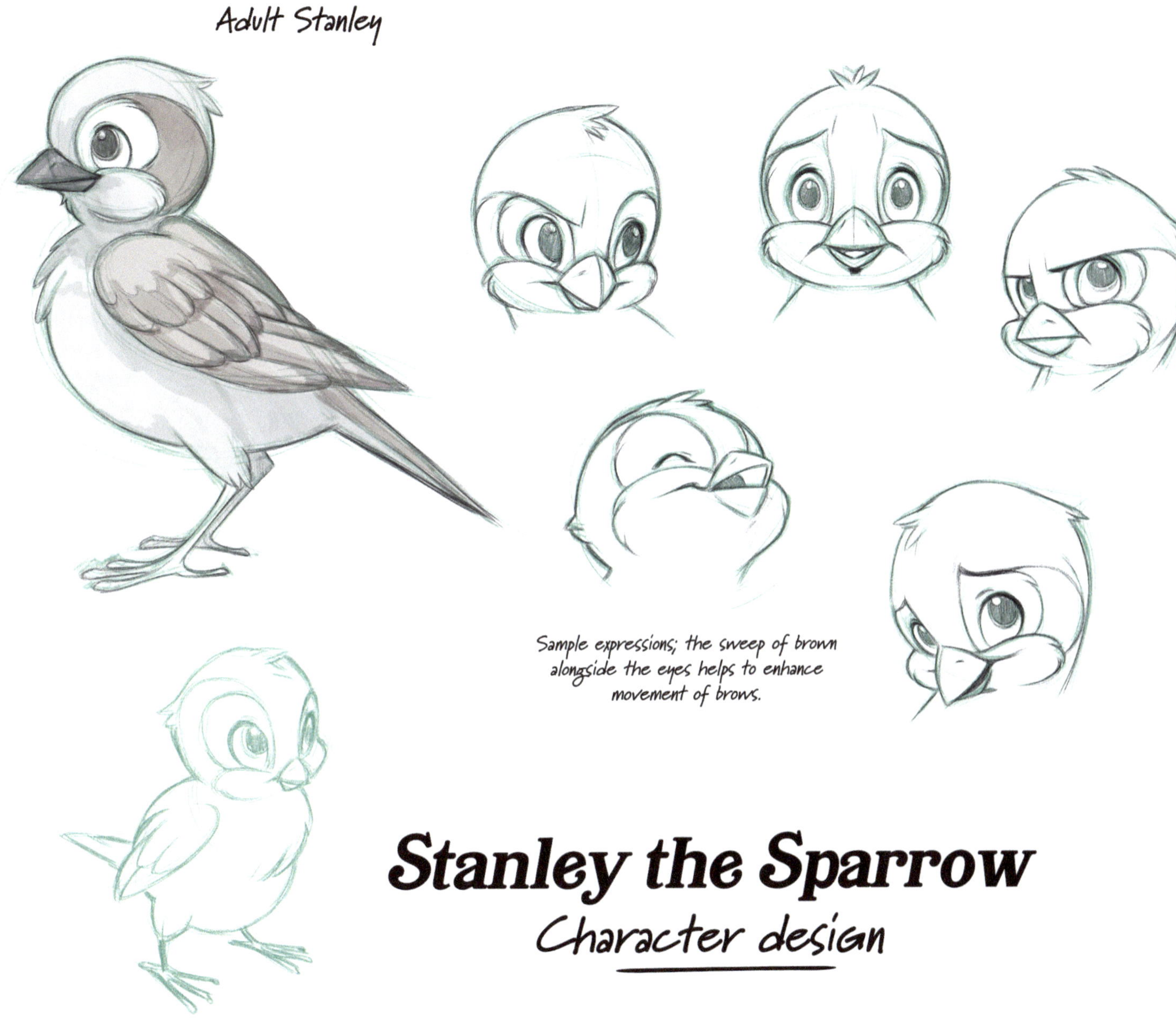

Adult Stanley
Sample expressions; the sweep of brown alongside the eyes helps to enhance movement of brows.
Stanley the Sparrow
Character design
Baby Stanley
© MHudson Illustration
11.11.2021